MATZO BALL SOUP

OR

THE BALLS THAT BOBBED
IN THE BROTH THAT
BUBBE BREWED

TO MY HUSBAND, STEPHEN, WITH LOVE AND
THANKS FOR HIS UNENDING SUPPORT.

TO LYNDA TRAILL, A GREAT ART TEACHER.

AND TO MY MATZO BALL SOUP EATERS:
NEIL, TORY, AND ZEKE.

TEXT COPYRIGHT © 1996 BY JENNIFER LITTMAN
ILLUSTRATIONS COPYRIGHT © 1996 BY JENNIFER LITTMAN
LIBRARY OF CONGRESS NUMBER 96-095405
ISBN NUMBER 0-9656431-0-7

MATZO BALL SOUP

OR

THE BALLS THAT BOBBED
IN THE BROTH THAT
BUBBE BREWED

BY JENNIFER LITTMAN

BRICKFORD LANE PUBLISHERS
BALTIMORE

This is the broth
That Bubbe brewed.

These are the balls
That bobbed in the broth
That Bubbe brewed.

This is the *matzo meal*
That was rolled into balls
That bobbed in the broth
That Bubbe brewed.

These are the eggs
That were bought by Zayde
And were added to the matzo meal
That was rolled into balls
That bobbed in the broth
That Bubbe brewed.

These are the carrots
That gave the flavor
And cooked with the eggs
That were bought by Zayde
And were added to the matzo meal
That was rolled into balls
That bobbed in the broth
That Bubbe brewed.

These are the bowls
All shiny and special
That contained the carrots
That gave the flavor
And cooked with the eggs
That were bought by Zayde
And were added to the matzo meal
That was rolled into balls
That bobbed in the broth
That Bubbe brewed.

This is the table
That was polished and set
On which were the bowls
All shiny and special
That contained the carrots
That gave the flavor
And cooked with the eggs
That were bought by Zayde
And were added to the matzo meal
That was rolled into balls
That bobbed in the broth
That Bubbe brewed.

These are the candles
That brightened the table
That was polished and set
On which were the bowls
All shiny and special
That contained the carrots
That gave the flavor
And cooked with the eggs
That were bought by Zayde
And were added to the matzo meal
That was rolled into balls
That bobbed in the broth
That Bubbe brewed.

This is the challah
Braided and warm
That was placed near the candles
That brightened the table
That was polished and set
On which were the bowls
All shiny and special
That contained the carrots
That gave the flavor
And cooked with the eggs
That were bought by Zayde
And were added to the matzo meal
That was rolled into balls
That bobbed in the broth
That Bubbe brewed.

This is the wine
Fruit from the vine
That went with the challah
Braided and warm
That was placed near the candles
That brightened the table
That was polished and set
On which were the bowls
All shiny and special
That contained the carrots
That gave the flavor
And cooked with the eggs
That were bought by Zayde
And were added to the matzo meal
That was rolled into balls
That bobbed in the broth
That Bubbe brewed.

These are the prayers of the Jewish people
That were said by the family
To thank God
For the candles, the wine, and the challah.

BLESSING OVER CANDLES

Ba-ruch A-tah A-do-nai
E-lo-hay-nu Me-lech ha-olam
a-sher kid-shanu b'mitz-vo-tav
v'tze-vanu l'had-leek
ner shel Sha-bat

We praise You, A-do-nai our God,
Ruler of the universe, who
has made us holy with commandments
and commanded us to kindle the lights
of Shabbat.

BLESSING OVER THE WINE

Ba-ruch A-tah A-do-nai
E-lo-hay-nu Me-lech ha-olam
Bo-ray p'ree ha-gafen

We praise You, A-do-nai our God,
Ruler of the universe,
Creator of the fruit of the vine.

BLESSING OVER CHALLAH BREAD

Ba-ruch A-tah A-do-nai
E-lo-hay-nu Me-lech ha-olam
ha-motzi lechem min ha-aretz

We praise You, A-do-nai our God,
Ruler of the universe,
Who brings forth
Bread from the earth.

And these are the grandchildren
Who kept Shabbat
And ate the balls
That bobbed in the broth
That Bubbe brewed.

GOOD SHABBAT!

A JEWISH TRADITION

Jewish families celebrate Shabbat after sundown on Friday
evenings. At this time, the family gathers for a festive meal.
Before eating, the family says prayers in Hebrew to thank
God for the light of the candles, the wine, and the traditional
bread that is called challah. Afterwards, they wish each other
a "Good Shabbat" and begin to eat. A soup that everyone
loves to eat is matzo ball soup. It is a delicious and easy soup
that children can make.

BUBBE'S MATZO BALL SOUP

INGREDIENTS :

4 (10 1/2 oz.) cans of chicken broth

4 cans of water

3 or 4 carrots

2 eggs

2 tablespoons of oil

1 package of matzo ball mix

DIRECTIONS:

BROTH

1. Pour the chicken broth and water into a large soup pan.

2. Cook on the oven at medium heat.

3. Peel and slice the carrots and add them to the broth.

4. Let the carrots and broth cook while you make your matzo balls.

BALLS

1. Break the eggs into a large bowl and stir them with a fork.

2. Mix in the oil.

3. Add the matzo ball mix and stir.

4. Put the bowl and dough into the refrigerator.

5. Let the dough cool for 15 minutes.

6. Shape the dough into walnut size balls.

7. Drop the balls into the broth.

8. Cook the matzo balls for 30 minutes in the broth.

9. Serve your matzo ball soup in bowls.

10. Now, enjoy your soup.

BUBBE'S GLOSSARY OF WORDS USED IN THIS BOOK

1. Bubbe=   Bubbe is a traditional Yiddish term for grandmother.

2. Challah =   Challeh is a braided bread that Jewish families serve for Shabbat.
              Traditionally, there would be two loaves of bread on the table at
              Shabbat. This was because women were not allowed to cook on
              the Sabbath.

3. Matzo =   Matzo is unleavened bread. Matzo is ground up into matzo meal
              and is an ingredient in matzo ball soup

4. Shabbat = Shabbat is a holiday in the Jewish community. It is the Jewish day
              of rest. It begins at sundown on Friday night and ends at sun-
              down on Saturday evening. Shabbat concludes with special ser-
              vices called Havdallah. Havdallah signifies the return to the work
              week.

5. Zayde =   Zayde is a traditional Yiddish term for grandfather.